Red Skies:
The Short Story

By
Shari Broyer

Rights and Disclaimers

This short story is a work of fiction. Any references to real people, events, establishments, organizations, or locales are intended only to provide a sense of authenticity, and are used fictitiously. All other characters, and all incidents and dialogue, are drawn from the author's imagination and are not to be construed as real.

Table of Contents

Acknowledgements...1

Author's Note..2

Red Skies...3

Also by the Author...26

About the Author...28

Acknowledgements

I wish to thank Dr. Andrew Carroll for his advice on I.V. solutions and their administration. (Andrew, I didn't ask you about the cleanup of the old gas station because I'm using my creative license in that area. If it's not what would really happen, well... the story wouldn't be the same if I changed it to fit the reality.)

I also want to thank fellow author, Sandra Leesmith, for being my beta reader and pointing out just a few areas that I needed to fix. Thanks so much, Sandra!

Author's Note

Dear Reader,

If, upon finishing this short story, you feel that you want more, that Emmie's tale has left much untold, don't be upset. This is the "teaser", if you will, for the novel to come. As I wrote this, I could see many places for expansion, but I wanted to get the short story out to use in a boxed set I am planning to put together for the holiday season.

So, please, be patient, and *Red Skies: The Novel* will also be available in the not too distant future.

If reviewing, please keep in mind that the length of this version is intentional, and please discuss its merits as a short story only. Thank you.

Feedback via my website contact form or the email address provided in the About the Author section at the back of this book is appreciated.

Sincerely,
Shari Broyer

Red Skies

Conneaut, Ohio 1989

"Red sky at night is a sailor's delight," Uncle Jim said, smiling at the flaming sunset over Lake Erie.

"And a red sky at morning is a sailor's warning," Emmie, his thirteen-year-old niece, completed the old saying. She pulled her fleece jacket more tightly around her as the day cooled along with the sun. The small sailboat rocked gently on the waves, and Emmie felt nothing but contentment.

She had no idea, at the time, that the saying actually came from the Bible, or that Jesus was warning the Pharisees that they were incapable of discerning the bad things that lay ahead. She had no inkling then, that these delightful days she shared with her beloved uncle were about to come to an abrupt end or that hardship waited just around the corner. Or that it would be years before she ever saw another red sky at night and looked at it with delight.

* * *

"Emmie, hustle up!" Her foster mother stood over the girl, rough hands shaking her out of a sound sleep. "The work ain't gonna get done with you lollygagging in bed all day. The store won't run itself, and I gotta go into the city. Get up now."

Groaning, Emmie hugged her pillow. She was so tired. It seemed like she'd barely gotten to sleep. She'd worked until nearly midnight last night, and she hadn't been able to fall asleep for yet another full hour, her legs and feet had throbbed so badly from being on them for that long.

Her foster mother grabbed the pillow out of Emmie's

arms and hit her with it. Emmie was lucky that was all Marion chose to use on her. "Up, I said, NOW!"

She stumbled out of bed and followed Marion to the kitchen. "Cornmeal mush, again?" she complained, wrinkling her nose at the smell.

"You'll eat what I put on the table, Miss, or go hungry. Now, sit down and don't dawdle. I need to drop you at the store in half an hour so I can beat the rush hour traffic into the city."

Twenty-five minutes later, Marion drove off for Cleveland, leaving Emmie to mind The Tackle Box, a small grocery/gas station/bait shop located along a lesser known road just off the highway that ran alongside the lake. Her foster mother was a teetotaler who didn't sell liquor. She had made Emmie fill out the consent for minors to work form and they both signed it; that's how she got away with having a fifteen-year-old minding the place.

The store had to be open by five a.m. for the convenience of those who fished the lake. Emmie yawned hugely and started the opening tasks, counting the cash in the till, stocking the cooler, shelving items to replace those purchased the day before and receiving goods from vendors before turning on the gas pumps, hitting the switch for the outside lights and flipping the sign to "Open." It wasn't hard work, but the days were extremely long and monotonous, dealing with grizzled old men who sometimes looked at her like they wanted more than they had a right to, and Emmie hated it. During the summers, she was the only one there from pre-opening at four a.m. until after closing at eleven, nearly twenty hours, at least three to four days per week. Heaven help her if she had to use the restroom and there was a crowd of customers to serve. It was a blatant violation of minor work laws, but who was there to notice—much less get involved enough to turn Marion in?

Emmie flung the case of breakfast burritos into the

cooler. The customers who shopped at The Tackle Box ate better than she did. She subsisted on that blasted cornmeal mush for breakfast, an overcooked hotdog or two for her midday meal (allowed only after the lunch bunch had bought up all the fresh ones), and whatever slop Marion decided to fix and bring her for dinner, most often pinto beans and—you guessed it—cornbread.

She was little better than a slave. She got paid nothing for all the hours of work except for the meager meals and her board. And Marion expected her to be grateful. Well, Emmie wasn't grateful; she was hateful. She hated Marion so bad, there were times she was tempted to rise in the middle of the night, take Marion's pillow and smother her with it as she lay snoring. Emmie loathed those snores. They sounded like a pig snuffling and snorting. That's what Marion was—a pig, a big, fat lazy hog.

Oh, why did Uncle Jim have to have that heart attack and leave her all alone? She'd been so happy living with him once she got over the death of her parents, who had died in an automobile accident when she was nine. Uncle Jim, Dad's brother, had been kind and wise and funny and fun. He'd made her do chores, yeah, but he didn't work her to death, and he gave her a generous allowance. And he never, ever raised a hand to her like Marion did.

Resentment smoldered in Emmie. It was only a matter of time before all that bitterness ignited into a conflagration of rage that would destroy everything, including Emmie herself.

* * *

It happened when Emmie forgot to take out the trash at home after work. Marion, angry as always at the slightest transgression, went into Emmie's bedroom with the belt she used to hold up her enormous jeans and walloped the sleeping girl with the buckle end.

Crying out as she awoke to vicious, biting pain across her cheek, Emmie's instinctive reaction was to fight back, but she held herself in check with great effort. She knew that crossing her foster mother in any way would only make it worse. "Get up and take the garbage out, you lazy thing!" Marion hollered.

Emmie stumbled out of bed to do her foster mother's bidding in her thin nightgown, barefoot. Marion went behind her and lashed her in the back with the belt buckle again just as Emmie put her foot on the first step down to the patio where the trash cans sat next to the back door.

Yelping, Emmie whirled and grabbed the buckle as it came at her a third time. She yanked on the belt, pulling Marion out of the door and down the last two steps with her as she did so. Marion lost her balance, stumbled and fell onto the concrete when her weapon flew out of her hands.

So enraged that she saw only red, Emmie turned the belt around and swung it with all her might, buckle end flying, at Marion's face as her foster mother struggled to her knees. All the heartache and suffering Emmie had endured at the hands of this horrid woman since Uncle Jim's passing two years ago spewed out of her like poisonous pus. Adrenaline and pent-up aggression enabled her to overpower her tormentor. She wielded the weapon again and again, not stopping until Marion, who'd been screeching and squealing like the pig she was, lay in a crumpled, silent heap at her feet.

Emmie, drained and spent, felt nothing. She didn't even bother to check to see if Marion was still alive. Stepping over her like she was a pile of refuse, Emmie went inside to the dresser in her tiny, Spartan room and began to stuff her meager belongings into her worn school backpack: the Bible Uncle Jim had given her that she'd never read but kept anyway because it had been his, photos of him and her parents, and the few articles of clothing she possessed that still fit her somewhat.

Then she went into Marion's room and rummaged through her purse, taking what cash she could find and the keys to the store. She grabbed a flashlight from a drawer in the kitchen on her way out.

Emmie left in the middle of the night and didn't look back.

* * *

Walking briskly, jumping behind a tree or bush or into the roadside ditch whenever one of the few cars that traversed the highway at that hour appeared, Emmie arrived undetected at the store around three-thirty a.m. She unlocked the door but kept the lights off as she disabled the alarm. Then, cupping the lens of the flashlight with her hand to diffuse the glare, she made her way to the safe and took out all the cash inside it. Marion usually made the bank run the following morning after a business day, so all the earnings from yesterday were still there.

Emmie went to the cash register next. She always emptied it at closing, but sometimes, a bill slipped under the money tray, and she'd forgotten to check for that last night. She smiled when she discovered another twenty to add to her funds and put it in the inner zip pocket of her backpack. Then she took some plastic grocery bags from under the counter and loaded them with all the good things she'd watched others buy and enjoy while she went without. She crept to the door, closing but leaving it unlocked behind her, and then struck out, bound for a destination as yet unknown.

* * *

Life after Marion hadn't been the picnic Emmie had thought it would be. Oh, yeah, at first she'd reveled in her freedom, had found a hidey hole in the woods where no one would detect her and spent two days gorging herself on candy, cookies, soda and chips until she was sick to her stomach. But by the third day, she had run out of sustenance and had to trudge breakfastless nearly ten miles to the next town to the southwest along Route 20. It was pouring rain, and she was without an umbrella, wearing for protection only the short, tight, fleece jacket she'd had since Uncle Jim was still alive.

She couldn't go back to Conneaut; that went without saying.

When she arrived in North Kingsville, soaked to the bone and shivering convulsively, Emmie found an inner stairway leading to a business on the second floor of a two-storey building and sat on the stairs for an hour or so while she dried herself as best she could. Thankfully, no one was around in the soggy weather. She pulled off her backpack and then her jacket and wrung it out on the sidewalk under the canvas awning outside. Back inside, she took off her shoes and sodden socks and squeezed the water out of them, forming a little puddle at the bottom of the stairs.

She turned her shoes upside down on the stair next to her feet and draped the socks over the stair beside her. She would have loved to take off the rest of her clothes and lay them out to dry, too, but she knew better than that, so she wrung the skirt of the despised, old-fashioned, secondhand 'sixties dress while she still wore it, enlarging the puddle. Then she took a plastic comb from her bag and ran it through her dark tresses over and over again until her hair stopped dripping. She fingered the scratch across her cheek and was relieved to find that it had finally healed enough that, even though the rain had softened and loosened the scab, it wasn't bleeding.

When she was dry enough, Emmie peered through the glass window in the door to locate the nearest market, and ventured back out. North Kingsville was a small town, smaller than Conneaut, and that was saying something. There was only one store nearby, situated kitty-corner from her across the street. Dashing through the rain, Emmie hid her backpack in an alley around the corner from the establishment after stuffing the money from its zipper pocket into her jacket pockets. She entered Recker's Groceries and Sundry in a breathless rush.

The proprietor, an old man with thinning white hair, looked up in surprise. "Afternoon, Miss," he said, his tone courteous as he quickly recovered his composure after her abrupt appearance, although he found it hard not to stare at the big scratch across the young girl's cheek. Kids were pretty wild these days. Perhaps she'd been in a fight with another girl with long nails.

"Hello," Emmie responded politely.

"Can I help you with anything?" he asked as he came around the counter.

"Do you have any umbrellas? Mine got messed up in all this wind and rain; it turned inside out and then the supports broke," Emmie lied. "My mom sent me in here to get another one."

The old man looked quizzically at her. "Oh? are you and your parents new in town?"

Nervousness made Emmie stammer, "N-no, w-we're j-just passing through. My mom's parked up the street. We didn't see the store until it was too late to turn into the parking lot." The subsequent lies slipped with less ease from her tongue, and she held her breath while she gauged the old man's reaction.

"Oh, well, then. Umbrellas are this way. You'll want a more expensive brand. Those cheap ones don't last worth a durn." He led the way to an aisle cap where a bunch of umbrellas stood in a round container. He took out one that was almost as long as Emmie was tall but looked sturdy, with a thick wooden handle, its framework covered in heavy, navy blue, water-repellant material.

"This one's twenty dollars, but if you take care of it, it will probably last at least that many years, if not more."

"The price is okay. Mom wanted me to get something that would last this time. Thank you very much. Can you take it to the counter for me while I get some stuff so my mom and I can make sandwiches? We're in kind of a hurry to get out west to visit my aunt, who's sick, and we don't want to take the time to wait at restaurants for our food to get done. We've been eating on the quick the whole way so far."

"Sure. Where'd you come from?"

"Connecticut," Emmie said promptly, having already come to the conclusion that the state would be a good one to use in case she slipped up and started to say, "Conneaut."

"And you're headed where?" The old man seemed only mildly curious, so Emmie felt safe in answering, "California." She would be heading in the opposite direction—to Canada via Buffalo—anyway. She'd also decided that since leaving Marion's. Canada was where people went to escape American authority.

"Oh, that's nice. I'll let you get on with your shopping then," he said and shuffled off toward the front of the store umbrella in hand.

Emmie went to the cooler at the back and removed a package of honey ham and another of provolone cheese slices. Then she browsed the aisles until she located some bread—the nice, soft, white kind. After all that cornbread, she wanted nothing grainy. Then she selected some mayonnaise and mustard, wavy potato chips, and a package of plastic cutlery. She brought these to the counter and set them down then went back to the cooler for some bottled water and Pepsis. From a rack by the counter, she took a copy of the *Conneaut Herald* and laid it down next to everything else.

When the old man raised a quizzical brow at the inclusion, she shrugged and said, "My mom likes to read. We stop at a park and have a picnic and she skims the newspapers from the towns we pass through while she eats."

There was no comment from the proprietor. Emmie had turned away to check on the weather so she didn't see the frown that made a new crease in his wrinkled brow.

After the old man rang up her purchases and double-bagged them per her request, Emmie carried the two bags outside, then opened the umbrella and set off down the street in the rain that had slowed to a drizzle. Figured. Now that she was mostly dry and had an umbrella, she didn't really need it. But Emmie had no doubt that she would need it again... soon. Weather off the lake was notoriously unpredictable.

Howard Recker, the owner of the store, opened up a copy of the *Herald* as soon as the girl was gone. When he read the front page article about a forty-five-year-old woman who'd been attacked by a man who used the buckle end of his belt, he wondered whether the woman in the paper was the girl's mother. Perhaps the girl had tried to intervene and had been struck, too? Maybe Marion Headle had sent her daughter in to shop for her today because she didn't want anyone to see the extent of her injuries. It made more sense that the single scratch on the girl's face had come from the sharp tongue of a buckle than from human nails, come to think of it. If another girl had scratched her, as he had first supposed, there would have been four marks across her cheek, not one.

Howard shook his head. What a shame that had to happen. It must have been so traumatic for them both. That's probably why they were leaving the area, to get away from the bad memories. Thank goodness he didn't have customers like the one who'd turned on Marion Headle. He shrugged and went back to work on the display of his product, a new brand of bubble gum with a fizzy inner center that would be a real hit with the kids.

At the intersection, Emmie hung a left and then

another right at the next block and zigzagged for two more blocks then retraced her steps until she came to the place where she'd first turned right and kept going straight so she ended up on the street behind the market. When she got to the end, she turned left and went into the alley to recover her backpack. Fortunately, it was still there. There wasn't anything in it worth stealing, anyway, but she didn't want to lose Uncle Jim's Bible.

From there, she headed to Route 84 and went south to Kingsville proper, a few miles away. By the time Emmie got to Kingsville, it was late afternoon, her arms were aching from carrying the groceries and she was starving. The rain had stopped completely, so she sat at a picnic table in the town square and ate. When she was full and rested, she took out the *Conneaut Herald*.

There was a front page story about the attack on Marion. The old witch obviously hadn't wanted it known that she'd been abusing her foster child because the article stated that Marion's attacker was unknown, a male wearing a ski mask who'd accosted her when she was taking out the trash at her home. He had knocked her down on the concrete and beaten her senseless with his belt, then robbed her of her cash and the keys to the store.

Marion claimed that the reason she didn't go to the police immediately was due to the beating. She'd been out cold for at least a day before she regained consciousness and had to heal enough to even make a call for another two days after that. It was speculated that the assailant was a customer who knew where Marion lived. It was unfortunate, the interviewing reporter commented, that Marion Headle hadn't installed surveillance cameras in her store. They would have captured the man on tape, and perhaps something would have given his identity away. Mrs. Headle said she'd be rectifying that oversight in the very near future. She also said she'd take new measures to ensure that she always set the alarm on the store door because the sounding of it might also have led to the apprehension of the culprit. Nowhere in the article was Emmie even mentioned.

Heaving a sigh of relief that Marion was alive and now she wouldn't have to face charges of murder, or even assault and battery, Emmie nonetheless knew that—if she didn't want to be picked up as a runaway and taken back to face justice at the hands of her foster mother—she'd have to be very, very careful from here on out. She had no idea that Howard Recker had connected her to Marion, however erroneously. She would have been doubly cautious had she known what a close call the visit to his store had been.

* * *

By the time she turned eighteen, on March thirty-first, 1993, Emmie had been homeless for nearly three years, constantly looking over her shoulder, always on the run. She never got to Canada. She had left Kingsville that day and made her way on foot along Route 84 to Kelloggsville then to Bushnell, and from there she crossed the border into Pennsylvania where she angled north to the shore of Lake Erie once again. She followed the shoreline for several days until she crossed into the state of New York.

Late summer had faded fast into an early fall, and though the gorgeous, flaming colors of the changing leaves cheered her somewhat, the relentless, cold rain off the lake did not. Nor did the fact that she was fast running out of funds, even though she had stopped eating at hamburger joints and started buying only from grocery stores and ate as little as she could each day to try to stretch her money farther.

The Tackle Box had only grossed about $750 on a good day because it wasn't strategically located. It was off Route 20 on a small side road and very few tourists ever found it. Even when they did, they often left in disgust when they discovered they couldn't buy six packs of beer to put in their coolers to enjoy while they fished. The store was frequented mostly by locals who needed a loaf of bread or a gallon of milk, or fishermen who'd gotten their drink elsewhere and just needed bait, stuff like that. The day Emmie left, it had grossed only $478, not counting the $20 she'd found when she checked the till. She was already down to $265, and she'd only been on the lam for eight days.

She determined then that she'd better give up the idea of Canada and head south before it got too cold, where at least she might survive out in the elements. Winters along the lake were often brutal; the wind chill factor could cause the temperature to plunge below zero by thirty to forty degrees, and heavy snow and ice storms were all too frequent. Emmie thought that by venturing into the farmlands, she could probably steal some leftovers from the harvests along the way, maybe even find a barn here and there to sleep in at night.

Her only goal was to keep from being discovered and hauled back to Marion's until she turned eighteen and was free at last.

* * *

Emmie recalled now how hard things had been—how she'd actually starved for a few days when her money had run out before she risked getting caught to beg an odd job at an isolated farm in exchange for a meal and a warm place to sleep for a night. How she'd gotten up in the middle of that night after four hours' sleep, leaving the warm bed behind and fleeing before the kind people decided they needed to let someone know where she was. How she'd had to beg, borrow and steal to stay alive, shivering in the cold, her threadbare clothes worn so thin she could see through them in places. How she'd patched the soles of her shoes with pieces of cardboard she'd found in a dumpster. How later she'd worn the filthy, but warmer, clothing she'd also found in the refuse, digging through it for aluminum cans and plastic and glass soda and water bottles to recycle. How she'd finally been reduced to eating food from the garbage, too.

She was still amazed she'd managed to survive it all. And throughout everything, when she'd gained and lost her meager possessions time and again, she'd held fast to Uncle Jim's Bible, though she still hadn't opened it, except to slide the photos inside it for safekeeping.

And now, in the early dawn hours of the morning on her birthday, she gazed at the lowering red sky and recalled the saying, "Red sky at night is a sailor's delight; red sky at morning is a sailor's warning." She cried then, to think that, even though she was free at last of the shadow of Marion Headle, she wasn't free of hardship.

"Red sky at morning is a sailor's warning." It was a sure sign that there were more trials ahead. "Oh, God," she cried aloud, shaking the Bible at the sky, "why are you punishing me?"

Emmie decided then that she'd head for Louisville. Now that she was eighteen, she'd surely be able to find a job there. "We'll just see about that red sky warning, God," she muttered. "You think you can treat me the way you have for the past three years and get away with it? You think you can take away the only person I had left on this earth, stick me with an abusive monster, then shove my face in the garbage and make me eat it after eating that pig's slop and get away with it? I'll show you!"

Pure rage burned within her. She gathered kindling for a fire, got it going, and, removing her photos, threw the Bible on top of the flames. A sharp pang ripped through her as she watched the red and orange tongues lick around the book like they were a dog and it was a juicy bone. "Sorry, Uncle Jim," she said aloud. "This isn't about you. *You* were wonderful to me. But God's been as terrible as you were great, and I just don't want to have anything to do with Him anymore."

At that instant, a crack of thunder reverberated across the skies, lightning flashed, and the clouds loosed buckets of rain. Emmie's meager fire sputtered out in less than a minute, and after a time of standing there, letting the cold water course down her body as hot tears coursed down her cheeks, she pulled the Bible from the smoking embers. Yelping, she dropped the book immediately and sucked on her blistered fingers. Yuck! They tasted awful. Emmie spat the bitterness from her mouth and held her lips open to the rain to rinse the nasty taste away.

"This doesn't mean I'm giving in to you, God!" she hollered. "It only means I can't give up the one thing I have left of the man who loved me—unlike YOU!"

After giving it time enough to cool, she hugged the sodden, charred Bible to her chest and ran from the woods, headed for cover in the abandoned gas station where she'd camped out for the past week. The rundown building squatted at the edge of the little town of Bedford, Kentucky.

When she got inside, Emmie huddled under the blankets in the nest she'd made for herself, trying to control her shivering. For some reason, she just couldn't get warm. She felt woozy, too. A sneeze escaped her, and then another. Great, just great. She was catching a cold, again. "Keep it coming, God! You're not going to win! I'll get even if it's the last thing I do! I hate you, you hear me? I HATE you!"

It was much more than a run-of-the-mill cold. For the next several days, Emmie was sicker than she'd ever been in her life. Her body was racked alternately with chills and fever, and she ached in every joint. She threw up repeatedly, and when there was nothing left in her stomach, she had the dry heaves for what seemed like eons. Then she got the trots, but couldn't even rouse herself from the pile of blankets to defecate in the far corner of the room, let alone go outside to the woods. Since the old gas station had no electricity or running water, there was nothing left to drink after the first day and she became so dehydrated that her skin peeled like she was sunburned. And when she started to cry, she stopped herself, knowing she was losing precious body fluids.

Emmie had never been so miserable or alone in her life, so, to the God she hated, she prayed to die. She almost did die. She came so close that the world around her shrunk to a grayish haze and what life she'd experienced thus far flashed like a bad movie before her eyes. Then, with her last ounce of strength, she picked up Uncle Jim's Bible, wanting to feel him close to her as she slid from this life into the next. She clung to it weakly—even though the burnt smell of it made her wheeze—and knew no more.

* * *

When she came to, warm sunshine was filtering in through the upper half of the station windows, the part that hadn't been painted over for privacy. Emmie could barely lift her head, and, after one attempt, she laid it back down on the old blankets that reeked of her own vomit and body waste. *Why am I still alive?* was her first thought, followed by, *I wish I were dead. Why didn't I die?*

The depression that engulfed her was so profound she dreamed up ways to kill herself once she was well enough to try—if she was ever that well again. A fierce hunger twisted her innards. She rationalized if she could just ignore it, she'd probably die, anyway. Her will to live almost extinct, Emmie closed her eyes and drifted away again.

The next time Emmie awoke, she felt herself being lifted and tried to struggle out of the arms that held her.

She dropped Uncle Jim's Bible in the process, and though she stretched her hand out as far as she could, she couldn't reach it. "Put me down!" she tried to say, but her tongue was thick and heavy and tasted like it was coated with tar. "Dah!" was all that came out.

"It's alright," a male voice soothed. "I won't hurt you."

Emmie felt a calloused hand gently smooth the hair out of her face, and she looked up into the bluest eyes she'd ever seen. The face was surrounded by a golden halo of hair. Together, they reminded her of a perfect summer day. Then, she lost consciousness again.

* * *

"I don't know what made me stop and take a look around, but I found her camped out at the old Shell station on the edge of town," Scott Lawrence told the emergency room doctor as he carried her back to the treatment area. "She's obviously been sick for days. The blankets she was laying on were covered in vomit and urine and feces just like her." His nose wrinkled in distaste. Only the knowledge that this girl was probably on the verge of death kept him from gagging now.

After ascertaining that the girl's fever had broken and she wasn't, in fact, in any immediate danger of dying, Dr. Silverman told his nurse, "Let's get an IV into her. Run one liter of Ringer's at full open, and then normal saline with twenty of potassium at 250. Get that going STAT, okay? After she's stable, clean her up, please."

"Yes, doctor, right away," the nurse hustled to comply, as anxious as he was to rid the area of the stench.

"Let me know when you're finished so I can give her a more thorough examination."

"Yes, doctor."

Dr. Silverman looked at Scott and jerked his head to

the left, "Come with me."

Scott followed.

When they were at the nurses' station, Silverman said, "You'd better go clean up, yourself. No telling what made her so sick. She could have hepatitis or some other druggie disease. Go on home now, shower and bag those clothes up to put in our bio hazard waste bins when you get back. We'll take care of her while you take care of yourself. I'll talk to you when you return."

* * *

Emmie moaned as gloved hands moved a wet, soapy cloth over the parched skin of her body. "Wah," she managed to get past her fat tongue.

The ministrations stopped, and a moment later a moistened square sponge on a stick was placed between her cracked lips. Emmie sucked it dry and begged for more. "Wah," she said again. A second helping was meted out. "Wah!" Emmie cried, insistent.

"Honey, I can't give you any more water right now. It might make you sick. You're getting fluids intravenously."

"Wah," Emmie said, eyelids still closed, weak tears escaping from their corners.

"I know sweetie, I know," the voice crooned as the bathing resumed. "You just hang in there, and we'll get you fixed up. It will take a few days, but you're going to be alright."

Suddenly, Emmie's eyes shot open and she tried to lift her head. "Bi!" she exclaimed hoarsely. "Bi!"

"What's that honey?"

"Bi!"

"I'm sorry, honey, I can't understand what it is you want."

"Bi..." Emmie's voice dropped to an exhausted whisper. "Bi..." She closed her eyes and let the tears flow.

* * *

"Can you go back to the station and clean it out?" Dr. Silverman asked Scott upon his return.

Scott nodded.

"Take everything outside and burn it, and then use bleach or some other disinfectant on the area where you found her. Until I get her blood work back from the lab, I don't want to take any chances. Her disease could be highly contagious. Wouldn't want an animal or another homeless person to pick it up and spread it around. Be sure to wear these while you're working, and if the gloves tear, wash your hands immediately." Silverman handed him a box each of medical gloves and face masks and some betadine solution. "And before you leave here, let's get some blood work on you, too, just to be safe."

After succumbing to a needle stick in the vein at the crook of his elbow and filling up the required number of vials with his blood, Scott left to do the doctor's bidding. He wasn't looking forward to the task, but someone had to do it. Dr. Silverman was right; leaving the mess could create a risk for the community.

Returning to the station armed with a box of long matches, some spray disinfectant, bleach, a bucket of hot soapy water, a broom and a mop, in addition to the stuff Silverman had given him, Scott propped the door open with a rock, and, donning some gloves and a mask, went to work. He'd brought a change of clothing with him so he could burn the ones he was now wearing along with everything else.

Holding his breath against the putrid air inside the station, he propped the door open with a big rock and started with the pile of blankets he'd found her lying on. Grabbing them up and away from his body, he carried them outside to a clear spot on the ground behind the building, far from the old gas wells. The wells were probably completely dry, but no sense asking for trouble. Then he gathered kindling and small branches from the woods behind the station, steepled them around and atop the blankets and set them ablaze before going back inside.

As he walked across the room, he tripped on something. He bent down and retrieved the item from the floor. It was a Bible. Hmmm... must've fallen from the blankets when he was taking them out. Strange—it looked like it had already been through a fire; the edges were crumbling and blackened.

Curious, he opened it. None of the interior had been harmed. The inscription inside read, "To Jim, Light and love of my life, second only to God, Yours forever, Geneva." What was that girl doing with someone else's Bible? He glanced at the flap opposite and found an address sticker:

James Matthew Whitson

1616 E. Main St.

Conneaut, OH 44030

Laying it down on a shelf and jogging outside to his truck, Scott pulled the soiled medical gloves off before opening the door of the passenger side. Then he popped open the little door under the dash and took out the pencil and notebook he always kept inside the compartment so he could copy the address before he added the Bible to the fire along with the ratty old backpack filled with worn clothing he'd also found.

Donning a new pair of gloves, Scott picked the Bible back up and opened it so he could jot down the information. Then closing the Bible, he took it outside, tossed it on the fire and went back inside to wipe down the shelf and sweep and mop out the area where the girl's things had been.

Keeping an eye on the fire every so often as he worked, Scott wondered about the girl. Where had she come from? Was she from Conneaut? If so, she was a long way from home. Perhaps writing a letter to that address would get some answers. He'd do it as soon as he got home for the night.

When he was through mopping, he sprayed the interior with disinfectant. Most likely, that wouldn't kill all the germs, but it would get the worst of them. Then he grabbed up the broom, mop and bucket and headed outside again.

Scott tossed the water on a barren patch of ground not too far from the fire. He knew the animals wouldn't go near it. They didn't like the smell of bleach, or fire. He wrung the mop out until it was nearly dry and threw it and the broom on the fire, then dug in the ground with the shovel he kept in the back of his pickup along with his other gardening tools until a fair-sized pile of dirt sat beside the hole.

He found an area inside the station where he could change and threw his old clothes on the fire. Once everything had burned sufficiently, he'd douse it with the dirt.

But as he stood by, waiting until the flames were gone and only glowing coals remained, Scott noticed that one item steadfastly refused to be consumed—the Bible. He'd heard of this happening before but didn't really believe it. Shaking his head, he used his shovel to pull the book from the embers. It couldn't hurt to keep it now. The heat would have killed all bacteria. Looked like this was the second time it had survived such treatment, so it must be pretty special.

* * *

A week later, Emmie was pronounced well enough to leave the hospital. The blood tests had revealed nothing, and it was suspected that a virulent stomach virus that had already died off was at fault. "No hepatitis, no HIV, no venereal disease, nothing to link her to drug abuse," Gardell, her doctor once she'd left Emergency, had informed Scott.

"Then I destroyed her few, pitiful belongings for nothing?" Scott exclaimed.

"No, not for nothing. That virus she had was highly contagious. Dr. Silverman was right to have you do that."

Even now, five days after finding out that the girl was contagious, Scott still felt really bad for burning everything she owned in this world. "Does she need a ride to the boarding house?" he asked Dr. Gardell now, aware that social services had procured a room for Emmie there. He'd kept tabs on her over the length of her stay and had visited her every day once he knew it was safe to do so.

"I think that's already been arranged, but you can go in to see her before she checks out, if you like."

When Scott walked into Emmie's room, a smile lit her face. She looked so different from the filthy bag of bones he'd carried in seven days ago. She'd filled out a little, due to the regular, healthy meals the hospital served; her skin glowed, and her dark hair shone with burnished highlights. She was dressed in a feminine flowered top with lace at the collar and a pair of jeans. On her feet were simple white canvas sneakers. Her hair had been cut and shaped by a volunteer cosmetologist so that her natural waves framed her face and made her green eyes pop. She wore no makeup, nor did she need any. Emmie—Emily Bridgette Whitson he now knew her name to be—was a beautiful girl.

"Hi there. I hear you're good to go now," Scott said as he advanced, hands behind him.

"Yep," Emmie said. "Thanks to you. I would have died if you hadn't found me when you did and brought me here."

"Aw shucks," Scott hung his head in mock bashfulness. Then he lifted his head and said, "I brought you something." He pulled the package from behind his back with a flourish.

"Oh, that's not necessary," Emmie protested.

"When you see what it is, I think you'll change your mind." Scott was aware Emmie had been asking for the Bible even before she was able to speak properly. But, he hadn't been willing to hand it over until he'd gotten an answer to his letter. Yesterday, he'd finally received it. A neighbor wrote that James Whitson had passed away five years previous, leaving his only surviving relative—his niece, Emmie, then aged thirteen—to be raised by the system. The neighbor had no idea where Emmie was now, but Scott did.

He handed her the crudely-wrapped package. As she plucked at the twine tied around newspaper comics, he told her, "I'm afraid you'll find it's a bit worse for wear. Sorry. I was instructed by Dr. Silverman to burn all your things when we didn't know what had made you so sick."

Emmie's hand stilled, "My Bible?"

"Yes, it's your Bible. Somebody Up There must really want you to have it. It wouldn't burn. I figured the fire killed all the germs, so I kept it and cleaned it up for you."

At Scott's words, a chill ran down Emmie's spine. She had tried to burn it, too, with the same results. Could it be possible? She tore open the wrapping, and turned to the inscription written by her Aunt Geneva years ago, before she died. Then Emmie did something she'd never done before—she closed her eyes and opened the tome to a random page. The first words her eyes fell upon when she opened them were, "It will be fair weather; for the sky is red."

As she read the rest of the passage, her eyes swam with tears. It was as if her beloved Uncle Jim was right there with her, and he was telling her that Someone Else was, too.

She just hadn't believed it before because she hadn't been able to "discern the signs of the times," signs that had been telling her all along that her heart was too hard. For the first time in three years, guilt for what she'd done to Marion washed over her and she bowed her head in shame. God had pulled her through that night and through so many more difficulties, even after she'd cursed Him and tried to destroy His word. He'd been with her, fair weather and foul, or she wouldn't be alive right now, wouldn't have such wonderful people around her, helping her to make a fresh start. And the handsome man standing in front of her was one of them.

Staring up into his kind, sky-blue eyes, Emmie suddenly was able to discern the future, a future that included Scott and their children, and a different kind of shiver, a warm one, raced down her vertebrae. She said, "Thank you. Thank you. Thank you. You don't know how much this means to me."

"Oh, I think I have an idea," Scott said, his lips quirking upward.

But truly, Scott hadn't a clue. He could only be thinking how much the book must mean to Emmie because it had been her uncle's. He didn't realize, as Emmie did at long last, that the Bible wasn't just special to her because it had been Uncle Jim's. It was special to her because it was God's. It was special because she'd found the red skies at night in it. It was special because she knew now that its pages held the promise of delight, of wonderful days filled with blazing twilights ahead of her.

Matthew 16:2-3 KJV

He answered and said unto them, "When it is evening ye say, 'It will be fair weather; for the sky is red.' And in the morning, 'It will be foul weather today; for the sky is red and lowering.' O ye hypocrites, ye can discern the face of the sky, but can ye not discern the signs of the times?"

Also by the Author

Jesus on a Park Bench

A middle-aged woman, alone and broke on the eve of Christmas Eve, finds new hope when she gives hope to a stranger.
This Amazon bestselling inspirational short story is striking a chord with readers; it remains in the top of its category nearly two years after its release on 12-24-12. Available on Amazon in Kindle and paperback formats.

The Neighbors

The neighbors are a constant source of ire for George, whose "Good Christian" halo slips further downward each time he has a run-in with them. His wife, Evelyn, seeks to make peace with the couple next door, but when she also has a "run-in" involving the wife, the chances of that become slim, indeed.
A short inspirational story, available on Amazon Kindle.

Buried Talents

Downtrodden Sara Avery once sang like a songbird, but no tune has escaped her lips in years. Taken for granted and verbally abused by her husband and her children alike, the only place Sara finds any solace is in her garden. One day as she hacks at the ground with a hoe like a serial killer with an axe, something flies up and hits her, literally forcing her to see things differently.
As Sara begins digging to uncover the self she's buried deep inside, she's met with resistance from her family. Now Sara has to find a middle ground somewhere in-between doing what's right for her and what's right for them. It will take a Power greater than herself to do it, though. When Sara also rediscovers her relationship with Him, even one of the worst things that could happen turns out to be a

miracle in disguise.

Like the Amazon bestselling inspirational short story, Jesus on a Park Bench, this novella by Shari Broyer with a holiday theme is also great reading for all seasons, not just at Christmas.

An inspirational novella available on Amazon in Kindle and paperback formats.

Petty Theft

The heretofore undisturbed gated community of Peaceful Pines is now up in arms over a rash of puzzling petty thefts. Nearly every house has been hit, but not one major ticket item has been taken, even though the thief is so professional the police have dubbed him the Cat Burglar. He moves so stealthily, no one ever hears him; there are no signs of forced entry; and not a single fingerprint is ever left behind. When the Cat Burglar targets her home while she's there, Cynthia Cambridge finds it downright scary, but that's not ALL she finds...

A short, fun, family-friendly mystery, available on Amazon Kindle.

About the Author

Shari Broyer has been writing since she was first able to wield a pencil. Her earliest awards: a 1st Place trophy for Creative Writing and certificate for First Runner-Up in Poetry at 8th grade graduation.

Formerly she was:

- Editor in Chief of KSU Ashtabula's literary magazine, *Kaleidoscope*
- Facilitator, Writers' Forum, Barnes and Noble, High Point, NC
- Host of *Writer's Digest* World's Largest Writing Workshop, Barnes and Noble, High Point, NC
- Published in various literary anthologies (most recently her poem "One-Eyed Jack" and "Squirrel" photo were featured in *Wild Edges—Manzanita, Poetry and Prose of the Mother Lode and Sierra*, released August 2010)
- Top 100 winner, *Writer's Digest* 2000 competition—Inspirational category, *Shades of Gray*
- Winner of author Terri Weeding's Little Ole Humor Contest
- Board Member/Newsletter Editor of Romance Writers of America, Desert Rose Chapter, Phoenix, AZ
- Finalist in the 2013 Minnesota RWA Romancing the Lakes Chapter Contest

Currently, Shari resides in Mesa, AZ and facilitates **Writers, Ink.** at Changing Hands Bookstore in Tempe, AZ. She is a member of the Christian Writers of the West chapter of American Christian Fiction Writers. As well, she belongs to the Scottsdale Society of Women Writers and the Desert Rose Chapter of Romance Writers of America. In 2013, she founded the To the Streets Project, which gives copies of her story, *Jesus on a Park Bench,* along with $5 gift cards for McDonald's, to the homeless in downtown Phoenix at Christmas. She recently joined the Mesa East Lions Club to further assist her community. She is also a manuscript editor for hire. She welcomes your feedback at **shariannegaylee@gmail.com**, and invites you to visit her website, **http://sharibroyerbooks.weebly.com**.